UNDERNEATH
A Collection Of Poetry And Couplets

HARSIMRAT DULAI

BLUEROSE PUBLISHERS
India | U.K.

Copyright © Harsimrat Dulai 2024

All rights reserved by author. No part of this publication may be reproduced, stored in a retrieval system or transmitted in any form or by any means, electronic, mechanical, photocopying, recording or otherwise, without the prior permission of the author. Although every precaution has been taken to verify the accuracy of the information contained herein, the publisher assumes no responsibility for any errors or omissions. No liability is assumed for damages that may result from the use of information contained within.

BlueRose Publishers takes no responsibility for any damages, losses, or liabilities that may arise from the use or misuse of the information, products, or services provided in this publication.

For permissions requests or inquiries regarding this publication, please contact:

BLUEROSE PUBLISHERS
www.BlueRoseONE.com
info@bluerosepublishers.com
+91 8882 898 898
+4407342408967

ISBN: 978-93-5989-665-6

First Edition: February 2024

Dedication

Dedicated To Anyone And Everyone, Who Inspired And Ignited My Inner Thoughts Seeking Voice.

Acknowledgements

I am immensely grateful to the publishing team who contributed to the creation of this book by transforming this collection into a tangible reality. I would also like to express my heartfelt gratitude to my readers, who find solace, joy, or reflection within these pages, your connection to my words is the greatest gift an author could receive.

Preface

"Underneath" is a heartfelt journey of emotions through a collection of poetry and couplets. The book indeed reflects the thoughts that brew underneath our human skin and yearn for everlasting echoes. In this book, the author invites you to experience the beauty of those thoughts in the form of poetry written in two languages. Each page is a tapestry of emotions, crafted to capture the essence of what lies beneath the surface. Through the author's eloquent verses, you will discover the magic of love and emotions in their purest form. Whether you are a hopeless romantic like the author herself, a lover of lyrical beauty, or someone seeking solace in the language of a poet, this book is for you! It's also a perfect opportunity for you to steal Instagrammable captions or share them with a loved one. Open the book, and let the words serenade you!

Prologue

In the depths of the human soul, where emotions simmer and thoughts dance in the shadows, there exists a realm unseen yet profoundly felt. It is within this realm that the essence of "Underneath" resides—a heartfelt journey of emotions waiting to be unearthed. The Author invites you to hear her thoughts as you flip through next few pages.

Contents

COPYRIGHT DECLARATION	II
DEDICATION	V
ACKNOWLEDGEMENTS	VII
PREFACE	IX
PROLOGUE	XI
CHAPTER 1 BREAKFREE	19
CHAPTER 2 BOTTLED MEMORIES	21
CHAPTER 3 CELESTIAL	23
CHAPTER 4 DOWN THE LANE	25
CHAPTER 5 DIFFERENT	27
CHAPTER 6 ETERNAL GARDEN	29
CHAPTER 7 FOREVER VIEW	31
CHAPTER 8 HIM	33

CHAPTER 9
HELPLESS   35

CHAPTER 10
HOME   37

CHAPTER 11
IN MY DREAMS   39

CHAPTER 12
LOST   41

CHAPTER 13
MY SPIRIT   43

CHAPTER 14
NOT AFRAID   45

CHAPTER 15
RAGE   47

CHAPTER 16
STARDUST   49

CHAPTER 17
SUN & SNOW   51

CHAPTER 18
THE LILY   53

CHAPTER 19
THE SKY   55

CHAPTER 20

TRAVELLER   57

CHAPTER 21
TROUBLE   59

CHAPTER 22
UNSEEN   61

CHAPTER 23
WAS IT?   63

CHAPTER 24
WHY?   65

CHAPTER 25
WITHOUT YOU   67

CHAPTER 26
THE MAN I NEVER MET   69

CHAPTER 27
UNREAL   71

CHAPTER 28
कशिश   73

CHAPTER 29
खो गया   75

CHAPTER 30
चेहरे   77

CHAPTER 31
बहाने   79

बारिश 81

CHAPTER 33
बरसात 83

CHAPTER 34
भुला दिया 85

CHAPTER 35
मेहजबीन 87

CHAPTER 36
रिवायत 89

CHAPTER 37
हक़ीक़त 91

CHAPTER 38
हवाएं 93

CHAPTER 39
आवारा 95

CHAPTER 40
एक शख़्स 97

Breakfree

In shadows deep, where echoes strain,
There lies a soul in silent pain.
Bound by chains of doubt and fear,
Yearning for freedom to draw near.

With every breath, a whispered plea,
To break the bonds and set it free.
Yet shackles forged from past regrets,
Hold tight, like unseen silken nets.

But in the heart, a fire burns,
A spark of hope that fiercely yearns.
For in the darkest of despair,
A glimmer of light dances there.

With courage bold, the spirit soars,
Defying chains, unlocking doors.
Through trials faced and battles won,
The journey's end has just begun.

For breaking chains is but the start,
To mend the wounds, to heal the heart.
To rise above and claim the sky,
And let the soul unfurl and fly.

Bottled Memories

You feel to me like childhood memories bottled up,

Bringing immense love, laughter, and warmth when opened up.

In each fleeting moment, a nostalgic symphony, Echoes of carefree days, a cherished reverie.

A kaleidoscope of colors, a whimsical parade,

Cotton candy dreams and lemonade.

You're the sparkle in the eyes of a gleeful child,

Running through meadows, free and wild

Celestial

I love his eyes for the hold the celestial abandoned,

But now gleaming again, just for me,

In the depths of his gaze, our stars align,

A cosmic connection, a celestial decree.

Down The Lane

I was walking down the lane, amidst the golden glow,
Where memories whispered, in a gentle ebb and flow.
Each step a tale, each breeze a whispered song,
In that tranquil path, where I truly belong.

Beneath the arching trees, their branches intertwined,
I traced the paths of yesteryears, etched in my mind.
With each familiar turn, a story did unfold,
In the whispers of the wind, tales of love retold.

The cobblestones beneath my feet, weathered and worn,
Echoed the journey of souls, from dusk till dawn.
Each pebble a witness, to the footsteps of time,
In that quiet sanctuary, where nostalgia does chime

I was walking down the lane, but it was more than that,
It was a journey within, where memories sat.
In the tapestry of time, where past and present blend,
I found solace in the lane, that seemed to have no end.

Different

My dark searches for your stars,

It's your name written in all my scars.

Behind my every smile, it's your face I see.

With you, I am my better self than I ever wanted to be.

We have been through it all, standing still tall.

My heart starts running your way every time you call.

I hear our heartbeats synchronising clearly.

With us, it's DIFFERENT & I never wanted something different this badly.

Eternal Garden

Your eyes met mine & a fire kindled in form of love,

Your hands held mine & it blazed.

Your lips touched mine & roses blossomed,

Your soul touched mine & it was an eternal garden.

Forever View

Walking through dark woods, on a cold winter night, I burnt the torch & saw things clear & bright.

While I'm on my way, I tripped over a rock & hurt my knee. I didn't stop even though I wanted to so badly.

Going far & deeper, I thought I lost my way, saw a smoking chimney & found a place to stay.

Little did I rest & begin again, I still had miles to cover, then it started to rain.

Tired, frustrated, I thought of quitting but I saved myself from losing.

Moments later, some magic happened,

A journey that was the hardest was now in the past

& I was standing in front of a FOREVER view that will last.

Him

He is like a warm cup of coffee on a wintery evening,

He is like summer breeze and windy rains,

He is a field full of roses and a spirit full of sunshine,

He is abundant like color blue and passionate like color red,

He is the color white, my soul finds peace with,

He is like moon holding the secrets of my night

And like sun, he washes off my darkness

He is like Christmas lights & New Year's fireworks,

He is like birthday balloons, glitter and confetti

He is everything my heart loves and my eyes look for.

Helpless

Rain pouring down into my veins & ocean breeze tumbling the hair, an infinite moment, not a story to tell.

Effortlessly, stealing my breath.

Like the words of my lover touching the soul & making me fall, helplessly, once & for all.

There again I'm stuck forever, forever in a moment, gazing into his eyes, eyes of a boy who smiles & sighs.

And yet again I find my self helpless, helpless to express.

What my heart is yearning to, to scream what I'm been dreaming to.

Home

You now have a home in my heart,

With doors left open & curtains drawn back,

With candles still burning & music still on.

In My Dreams

In my dreams you are so close,

So close, that I can hear you breathing.

So close, that your scent smothers me.

So close, that your smile brightens me up.

So close, that the world doesn't bother me.

So close, that you seem an almost reality.

So close, that I start losing my sanity.

So close, that I cherish every moment spent.

So close, but in waking, it's all just lent.

Lost

To the rain drops dancing in the dark of night,

And the wild jasmine far from my sight,

It's befuddling to pick one that's right.

The one that echoes or the one that's still,

The one that torments or the one that's tranquil.

Gazing into the distance, lost and astray,

I buried my thoughts for yet another day.

My Spirit

My mind is my throne,

& I sit their patiently.

My heart is a racecourse

& my spirit dances there wildly.

My thoughts are like shooting stars,

& in my blood they burn brightly.

Not Afraid

Even though I am waiting for the sun to rise again,

I am not afraid of the night,

Its peaceful & preparing me for the day.

Even though I am waiting for the birds to sing again,

I am not afraid of the silence,

It lets me hear what my heart has to say.

Rage

Like the wild winds ceasing upon touch of strong trees,

Like the giant ocean waves fading away into the lap of sea,

He calmed my rage and set my mind free.

Stardust

Two souls rhymed over stardust to become one star again,

A celestial dance, a love that none could feign.

In the cosmic embrace, their energies entwined,

A symphony of galaxies, a union designed.

Sun & Snow

My anger is like snow, it melts & disappears.

My love is like sun, its warm & eternal,

My patience is like sand, can't hold on to it,

My agitation is like ocean, holding it into depths abyssal.

The Lily

In the water, floats the lily,

Hoping to reach the shore.

Smiling at the stillness of lake,

Dreaming of having more,

More of life, more of air, more of a rhythm,

Balancing amid storms, an attempt to fathom.

To learn & grow wise before time arrives of its demise,

Little did know little lily,

She was rooted there to bring hope,

Hope to all looking for something like her grace,

UNDERNEATH

Something exactly like her to embrace.

But still floats the lily, the lily unknown,

Hoping to reach just the shore.

UNDERNEATH

The Sky

Don't call me the moon, don't call me the sun.

If you must, please call me the sky.

They both appear in me

& you don't get to choose just one.

Traveller

Magical, oh so magical you seem,

I've been wanting to run away from your eyes' gleam.

It was indeed a chain reaction leading me to you,

There you were standing tall under the sky so blue.

Your flesh was a song & your touch the words,

I sang along, danced along, like a traveller of familiar roads.

Now that I know it was all a lie & not even a dream to be partially true,

I still cherish it for the spark it sets within me

& all the blazing hues.

I'll be your lover for the time you live & I'll be your lover for the time after.

UNDERNEATH

This love of mine is my killer & this love of mine is my savior,

Only for me to love you more & better.

Trouble

You smell like trouble but I want to devour you still,

A taste of allure, and a daring thrill,

A hint of mischief and all my senses to fulfill.

Unseen

Liquid galaxies allied with sunflower fields,

Such a mind is madness yet beautifully at peace.

It sings the songs in hues of phosphenes,

And sits in silence admiring the unseen.

Was It?

Was it a wind or a breeze?

Was it a storm or hurricane?

Was it a tide or a flood?

Was I wise or naive?

Was it destroying or evolving?

Why?

The moon & the stars are hung over the sins of the sun.

The sky is mourning on loss of daylight.

The night is intoxicating, the flowers aren't blooming,

And you are wondering why universe is not listening?

Without You

May you be the sea & I be the tide.

May I exist within but not without you.

May you be the road and I be the traveller,

May I get it lost when you aren't there to walk me through.

The Man I Never Met

You mended aspects I wasn't aware required repair,
In moments of joy and playful banter, we'd share.
It all felt like a utopia, a dream so appealing,

You, my guiding star, remained constant with my lunar dealings.
A radiant spark, surpassing the brilliance of noon.

Yet, despite this connection, we never met, and I swoon.
I question why fate kept us apart, oh, how I sigh.

A perpetual void you left, one I won't allow another to occupy.

Unreal

His gaze, adorned with beautiful brown hues,
Though I never truly met its embrace.
Those lips, resembling Cupid's bow,
Though their touch eluded my grasp.
The occasional smile that graced his face,
Yet I never experienced its genuine glow.

The mark on his hand, a unique trace,
Though my fingers never traced its form.
How does one fall for someone unreal,
Yet, with him, the intangible felt remarkably warm.

In his presence, the infinite became tangible,
A surreal connection that felt undeniably real

कशिश

हम कहां थे बातों में फसने वाले

वजह बनगई उनकी आंखों की कशिश

ना तब चला था बस मेरा ना चलता आज है

करलू रिहा होने की कितनी भी कोशिश।

मेरे दिल के ख्वाबों को

उसकी हकीकत की थी तलाश

अपनी आंखों से लिया ताराश।

खो गया

चांद अगर तेरा खो गया रात के अंधेरे में कहीं
तू रोशनी सूरज की ले कर उसे ढूंडने तो जा

ना मिले अगर दिन के उजाले में सरेआम
तू पर्दा कर बादलों का उसे मना ला

सितारों से बातें कर, रातों का सफर बना
दिल की धड़कन में बसा, उसे अपना खुदा बना

रोशनी की किरणों से लिपटे तेरे ख्वाब
बादलों को छूने की कहानी को अपनी बना ला।

चेहरे

चेहरे अलग शख़्सियतें वही
लोग अलग जज़्बात वही
बातें अलग इरादे वही
कहानी अलग वादे वही
जो ना बदला ना समझा
ना जिया ख़ुद के लिए कभी
मै वही दिल वही
दर्द वही शिकायत वही।

बहाने

तू ग़ज़ल कोई ऐसी है जिसे सिर्फ हम पड़ पाते हैं।
आँखों ने सुनी थी आँखों की
वरना जुबान के बहाने हमें भी आते हैं।

हर गुनगुनाहट में तेरी महक है,
बिना शब्दों के, तेरी धुन को हम पहचानते हैं,
किताबों में छुपी तेरी रहस्यमयी बातें,
हर इशारे में, तेरी कहानी हम पढ़ पाते हैं।

बारिश

सर्दी की धूप सी चाहत बदल बारिश में गई

भीगने को हैं अरमान अब भी

मगर वो पहले जैसी ख्वाहिश नहीं।

दिल की गहराइयों में उठता है एक एहसास नया

बारिशों की धुन में, है एक इंतजार नया

नया है इश्क़, नया अंजाम होगा

बेकसूर दिल फिर बदनाम होगा।

बरसात

मौसम बरसात का है,

आँखें तो नाम होंगी ही

चाँदनी रात का है मज़ा अगर,

सितारों की बातें भी होंगी ही

खोए ख्वाबों की दुनिया में, साथ उसका मिल जाये जो,

बेरंग रातें मेरी हसीं होंगी ही।

भुला दिया

मैं वो राही हूं जिस की मंज़िल ने लौटने का रास्ता भुला दिया,
मत पूछना मेरा सफ़र कैसा था,
सफ़र मेरे में मैंने ख़ुद को भी भुला दिया।

हवाएं बातें करती हैं अब मेरे खोए साए से,
मैं डरता था जिन राहों से, देख आज इश्क़ भी किया उस चौराहे पे।

मेहजबीन

गुलाबों की खुशबू से इत्र सभी बनाते हैं,

उसने बनाया एक ख्वाब हसीं।

ख्वाबों में मोहब्बत की बातें सभी कर जाते हैं,

उसने खामोशियों में महकाया शबाब मेहजबीन।

रिवायत

अजीब रिवायत है ज़िन्दगी की,
जीते उनके लोए हैं जिनपे मरते हैं,

उनकी राहों में पल भर के लिए खुद को खो देते हैं,
सलामत रहे वोह
सज्जदे उन्ही के करते हैं।

अजीब रिवायत है ज़िन्दगी की,
जीते उनके लोए हैं जिनपे मरते हैं।

हक़ीक़त

बदला वक़्त मेरे लिए कुछ ऐसा

ले आया नए जज़्बात कई

बतादें तुझे हक़ीक़त एक, ए हसीन

रातें ख़ामोश हैं बेशक मेरी

मगर बर्बाद नहीं

इनमे स्कून है अब आज़ादी का

तेरी दर्द भरी याद नहीं

मुझे तुझ से जो इश्क़ था उसकी हसरत नहीं, फरियाद नहीं।

हवाएं

मेरी इजाज़त के बिना तुझे छूती जो हवाएं हैं

इन्हे पता देना कभी मेरे अंदर के तूफ़ान का।

तेरी हर आहट पर, हर कदम पर,

मेरा साया तेरे साथ है।

जो कभी ना छूटे,

तूने थामा वो हाथ है।

आवारा

फिर यूं शामें मलंग हुई
दिल घूमा आवारा किसी की गलियों में
फिर रातें हसीन हुई
हमें चाहा किसी ने करीब से।

सितारों की रोशनी, चाँदनी का साथ
हमें चाहता रहा कोई, ख्वाबों की बात
रात के संग हुई एक नई मुलाकात
हमें चाहा किसी ने करीब से।

एक शख़्स

एक शख़्स गुलाब सा
मुझे इत्र की तरह मिल गया
मुरझा गया चाहे फूल वो
खुशबू की तरह यादों में रच गया।

उसकी मुस्कान में छुपा सुकून है
दिल को भाए है वो मुस्कान
हर दर्द ओढ़ लिया है उसने ख्वाबों से
जैसे रात बूंदों में छुपा हो सफर-ए-जहान।

www.ingramcontent.com/pod-product-compliance
Lightning Source LLC
LaVergne TN
LVHW061344080526
838199LV00094B/7353